The
Foolish
Giant

The Foolish Giant

BRUCE AND KATHERINE COVILLE

A Harper Trophy Book
Harper & Row, Publishers

Library of Congress Cataloging in Publication Data

Coville, Bruce.
  The foolish giant.

  Summary: The adventures of a not very bright but friendly giant named Harry.
  [1. Giants—Fiction] I. Coville, Katherine. II. Title.
PZ7.C8344Fo   [E]   77-18522
ISBN 0-397-31800-6

  (A Harper Trophy book)
ISBN 0-06-443229-7 (pbk.)

Published in hardcover by J. B. Lippincott, New York.
First Harper Trophy edition, 1990.

TO GRAMMA AND GRAMPA CHASE
WITH LOVE

Once upon a time there was
a giant whose name was Harry.
He was not very bright.
He was friendly.
He was brave.
And he was kind.
But he was not very bright.

Harry liked to do things for the
people he lived with. In summer
he would make pine trees into fans
to cool off the town . . .

8

. . . and use his bathtub to
water people's gardens.

He even held up the steeple while
the town church was being built.

But the best thing that Harry did was to keep the wicked wizard who lived on the hill from taking over the town.

Only nobody knew about this, because the wizard never dared to make trouble as long as Harry was around.

Sometimes people got angry with
Harry when he tried to be helpful.

Like the time he helped Will Smith
dig for fishing worms. . . .

And the time he helped
with the wine-making. . . .

And worst of all, the time
he picked some flowers
for the mayor's wife, and
they turned out to be the
mayor's best apple trees.

17

"Harry, you great fool!" cried
the mayor. "I'm sick of your
stupid tricks! Why don't you
get out of town?"

"That's right!" cried the people.
"All you do is cause trouble!"

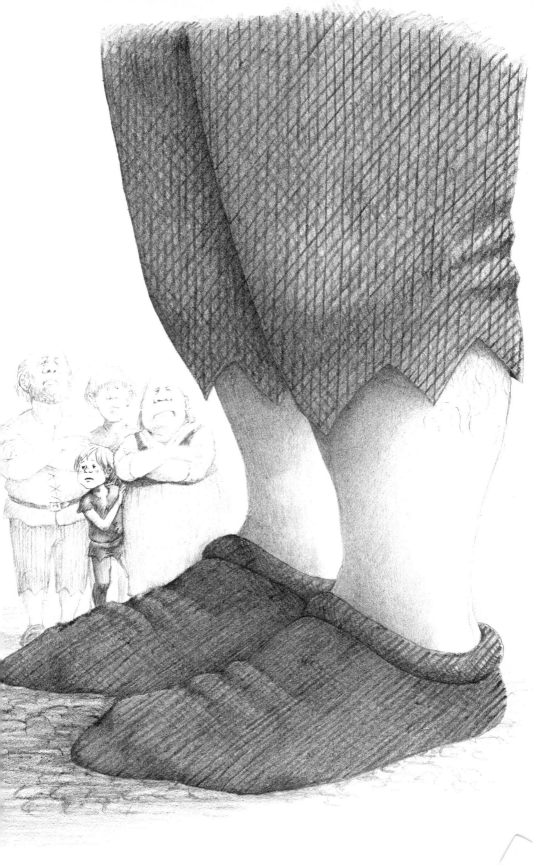

Harry thought his heart would
break. But then he thought about
all the messes he had made.
Maybe the people were right.

Wiping away his tears, Harry
went home and packed. Then he
moved to a cave far from town.

But Will Smith followed him
to see where he went, because
he didn't want to lose his friend.

When the wizard saw Harry go
he rubbed his hands with glee.
Now there was nothing to stop him
from taking over the town.

First he turned the mayor's wife
into a cow. The spell only lasted
for three hours. But it proved
what he could do.

Next he told the people he wanted half of all they had, or he would turn them into stone toads. They knew he could do it, so they gave him what he wanted.

But he was greedy, and soon he
wanted more . . . and more . . . and
more!

Before long there was nothing left
to give him.

When the people told the wizard
this he was very angry. He told
them they had until sunset to find
more, or . . . poof! *Stone toads!*

What could they do? They huddled in their homes and waited for the end.

Except Will. He went to get Harry.

Harry was sitting in front of
his cave, shaving.

"Harry, you've got to help us!"
cried Will. "The wizard is going
to turn us into stone toads!"

Harry didn't even finish shaving.

He picked Will up and ran for town.

It was almost sunset when Harry
reached the town. Time was running
out.

There was a flash of light
from the tower. The wizard
was getting his magic ready.

"Harry, you've got to do something!" cried Will.

Harry put Will down.

He went to stand in front of
the town. "I'll let the magic hit me,"
he thought. "After all, I'm only a
foolish giant. Who cares if I turn
into stone?"

"Harry, come back!" cried Will.

When the people heard Will yelling
they peeked out their windows.
"Harry, come back!" they cried.

There was another flash of light from the tower.

The wizard had thrown his magic.

It struck Harry right above his heart.

Everyone began to cry.

But the magic had hit Harry's
shaving mirror. It bounced back
to the tower and turned the wizard
into a stone toad.

The people could hardly believe it.
"Harry beat the wizard!" they yelled.
"Hurray for Harry!"

Harry opened one eye and then
the other. He looked around. He
wondered if he was stone yet.

He wiggled his fingers.

He touched his nose.

And then he smiled.

Harry never did figure out
what had happened. But everyone
said he was a hero.

They even gave him a medal.

Harry was so happy
he started to cry.

Of course, Harry still did some
foolish things.

But now most people thought
it was because he was busy
thinking up more clever plans.

And the rest of the people,
who knew that he was just as silly
as ever, loved him anyway.

After all, he was friendly,
brave, and kind.

And, of course, they
all lived happily ever after.

BRUCE COVILLE, an elementary school teacher, has worked as a gravedigger, a toymaker, a salesman, and an air freight agent. KATHERINE COVILLE, also a toymaker, once made a dollhouse—complete with furniture and doll—inside a hollowed-out acorn. The Covilles live in Phoenix, New York, with their two children. *The Foolish Giant* is their first book.